For Isla May

BLOOMSBURY CHILDREN'S BOOKS
Bloomsbury Publishing Plc
50 Bedford Square, London, WC1B 3DP, UK

BLOOMSBURY, BLOOMSBURY CHILDREN'S BOOKS and the Diana logo are
trademarks of Bloomsbury Publishing Plc

First published in Great Britain 2018 by Bloomsbury Publishing Plc

A catalogue record for this book is available from the British Library

ISBN: HB: 978-1-4088-9818-5 PB: 978-1-4088-9360-9

2 4 6 8 10 9 7 5 3 1

Printed and bound in China by Leo Paper Products, Heshan, Guangdong

To find out more about our authors and books visit www.bloomsbury.com and sign up for our newsletters
To find out more about Katie Abey visit www.katieabey.co.uk

WE WEAR PANTS

KATIE ABEY

BLOOMSBURY
CHILDREN'S BOOKS
LONDON OXFORD NEW YORK NEW DELHI SYDNEY

We Wear Pants

Which animals are **wearing** pants? Find your **favourites!**

We Wear Hats

Choose a hat and find your **favourite** animal.

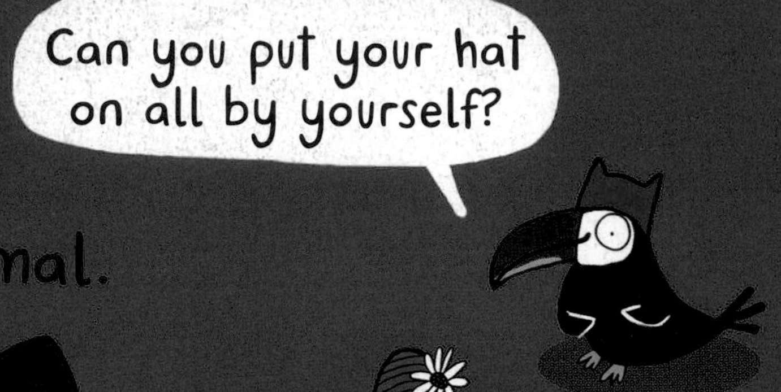

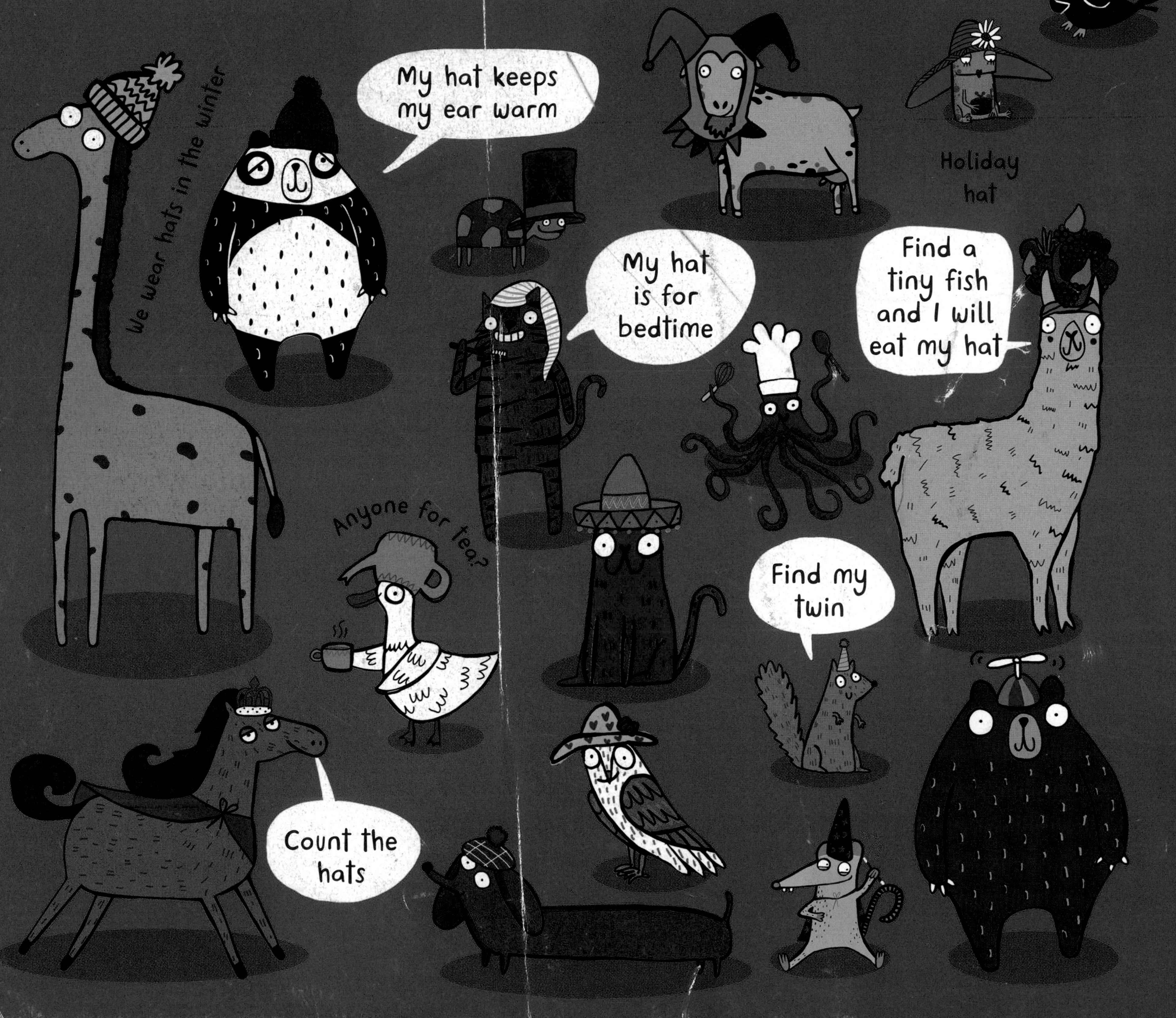

We Wear Socks

What are these animals wearing?

Socks are for feet

Croc in a sock

Urgh smelly!

Not me, I'm wearing shoes!

Twinkle socks

OOPS! Too big!

Who is on my sock?

We Wear T-shirts

What are all the animals **doing** at the fair?

We Wear Pyjamas

Goodnight animals. Don't **forget** your pyjamas!

We All Get Dressed